10 X
1 - 2011

Murder, My Tweet

Chet Gecko Mysteries

Murder, My Tweet

Bruce Hale

HARCOURT, INC.

Orlando • Austin • New York • San Diego • Toronto • London

www.HarcourtBooks.com

Library of Congress Cataloging-in-Publication Data
Hale, Bruce.
Murder, my tweet: from the tattered casebook
of Chet Gecko, private eye/by Bruce Hale.
p.   cm.
"A Chet Gecko Mystery."
Summary: Detective Chet Gecko and his associate,
Natalie Attired, take a case trailing what they think
is a cheating boyfriend but are instead led to a school
mystery that involves blackmail and robots.
[1. Geckos—Fiction.   2. Animals—Fiction.
3. Schools—Fiction.   4. Extortion—Fiction.
5. Robots—Fiction.   6. Humorous stories.
7. Mystery and detective stories.]   I. Title.   II. Series.
PZ7.H1295Mu   2004
[Fic]—dc22   2004003597
ISBN 0-15-205012-4

Text set in Bembo
Display type set in Elroy
Designed by Ivan Holmes

First edition
A C E G H F D B

Printed in the United States of America

For Steve Malk, ace agent and gecko true believer

A private message from the private eye . . .

Life is brimming with mysteries. Like, if you toss a cat out of a car window, does it become kitty litter? If a cow laughs, does milk come out her nose? And if I'm a nobody, and nobody's perfect, does that mean I'm perfect?

I wonder about these things. That's my job. I'm Chet Gecko, Private Eye, and mysteries aren't just my bread and butter, they're the maraschino cherry on my triple-decker banana-slug sundae.

But to me, friendship is no mystery. Having a buddy you can count on is one of the finer things in life—right up there with all-you-can-eat buffets, summer vacation, and owning a comic book collection as big as a house.

Some say that a friend in need is . . . a pest indeed. Not me. 'Cause when it's your partner in trouble, that's a whole 'nother can of chocolate-covered worms.

A routine case took a turn for the worse when my best pal and partner, Natalie Attired, was framed like a four-million-dollar Rembrandt and booted out of school. I tackled the case for free.

But clearing her name wasn't as easy as potato-bug pie. As I traced the thread of clues, it grew longer and wider, until I found myself unraveling a conspiracy big enough to make a bib for a bronto-saurus. It led me to a criminal mastermind so brilliant, he made Einstein look like a dim bulb.

Did I tough it out to the bitter end, despite danger to life and limb? Let me put it this way: Even though we geckos may be green-skinned, we can be true-blue, too.

1

Sneak and Ye Shall Find

Never take on a wacko as a client. It wastes your time, and it annoys the wacko.

Somehow I had forgotten this. And so, recess found me tailing a parakeet's boyfriend to see if he'd been stepping out on her. (That's detective talk for seeing another dame on the side. And a *dame* is a girl. And *on the side* is . . . on the side.)

I shadowed T-Bone LaLouche through the halls of Emerson Hicky Elementary. Like any good detective, I used kids, bushes, and the odd teacher as cover. (And believe me, we have plenty of odd teachers.)

T-Bone LaLouche was a lean and shifty ringtail. Ringtails have a cat's body, a fox's face, and a raccoon's tail that's been dipped in goo and slammed in a door.

Oh, and one other thing: If you startle them, they give an ear-piercing shriek and shoot this funky musk from their butts.

Don't ask me how I know that.

I watched as T-Bone stopped near the library to chat with a simpering mole in a tutu. Heads together, they seemed awfully chummy. Could this be his extra-credit baby-cake?

When I leaned around a skreezitz bush for a better look, T-Bone suddenly glanced up. I dived for cover—*kronch!*—right into the bush.

Through the spiky leaves, I could see the ringtail frowning my way, but he went back to his confab. Soon, the mole waved toodle-oo and toddled into the library. T-Bone took to his heels.

I tagged along.

In the hall by the cafeteria, the ringtail approached a fluffy European rabbit. (I could tell she was European by her spiffy scarf and her world-weary ways.)

Miss Fluffy leaned against a pole and toyed with her whiskers. T-Bone cozied up. She passed him something—a love note?—and they giggled like a couple of teenage girls at a Brad Spitt movie.

Man, this guy wasn't just two-timing my client; he was *three*-timing her.

Sensing something, T-Bone raised his head and started to turn.

Fa-zoop!

I scrambled up the wall, out of sight. In my racket, sometimes it pays to be a wall-crawling lizard.

I crept along quietly. Then my foot slipped. *Strange.* We geckos can scale almost anything, including glass. I shook the foot and crawled closer . . . just across from the cuddly pair.

A strange sight distracted me: squatty machines being wheeled into the cafeteria. And they were wearing what looked like . . . aprons? Was head chef Mrs. Bagoong getting some new cooking gizmos?

I shook my head. *Better focus on the job at hand.*

Miss Fluffy was saying, ". . . after you do me this favor, you and I can . . ."

Someone had taped a WET PAINT sign to the pole she was leaning on. Silly rabbit. Didn't she know—

Fffffwwip!

Suddenly, everything slipped. I scrabbled desperately, clawing a paper sign from the wall. It read, WET PAINT.

Duh. The pole hadn't been painted; the wall had.

"Whoooah!" I cried, plummeting like a duck after a pond-scum sandwich.

SKREONCH! A shrub broke my fall.

"*AAIIEEE!*" T-Bone shrieked, like an air-raid siren singing opera. Under his scream, something went *ffrappp!*

The rabbit and I clapped our hands over our ears. A second later, we covered our noses instead.

The ringtail had blasted a paint-peeling musky stench, fouler than a roadkill casserole. It spread down the hall, clearing kids and teachers with its potent funk. Miss Fluffy fled.

Eyes watering, I coughed and hacked and staggered to my feet.

With as much dignity as he could muster, T-Bone stood tall and glared at me. "It's your own fault," he said. "Maybe you shouldn't startle kids like that."

"Maybe *you* shouldn't have had the cabbage-and-cheese breakfast burrito."

The ringtail snorted. "Oh yeah? Maybe *you* shouldn't sass someone bigger than you." He loomed over me.

"Oh, really? Maybe you shouldn't be two-timing your girlfriend," I said.

"My *girlfriend*?" he asked.

"Yeah, your bubby-cakes, your doll-face, your smoochie-poo. Anne Gwish?"

His face froze. "Anne *what*?" said T-Bone. "Who's she?" He stalked away.

Still holding my nose, I stumbled in the opposite direction.

From above, a *clap-clap-clap* reached my ears. I glanced up.

It was Natalie Attired, my spiffy mockingbird partner. An ace investigator, she thought she was quite the joker (but she was really just a card). Perching on the roof's edge, Natalie looked me up and down, from my paint-smeared feet to the twigs in my hat.

I held up a hand. "I know, I know. I'm scratched and filthy, and I smell like a ringtail's butt."

"So, other than that," she said, "how was your day, dear?"

2

A Mole in One

Natalie and I retreated to a corner of the playground. While wiping paint from my hands and feet with paper towels, I told her about our new case.

Or I tried to, anyway.

"Hey, Chet," she said, "why do seagulls fly over the sea?"

"Look, I'm cranky, and I just blew a tail job. This is no time for jokes."

Natalie smiled patiently. "Why do seagulls fly over the sea?" she repeated.

I sighed. "Okay, why?"

"Because if they flew over the bay, they'd be bagels!" Natalie cackled.

I hated to admit it, but that was almost funny. For a bird joke.

"Pretend I laughed," I said. "*Now* can I tell you about our crazy client?" I filled her in on why Anne Gwish, the parakeet, had hired us.

Natalie raised a wing feather. "Wait, so she thinks her boyfriend's two-timing her?"

"Yup," I said.

"And she hired us to prove it?"

"Uh-huh."

"But he doesn't even *know* her?"

"That's right."

"You're not kidding," said Natalie. "She *is* crazy."

I shrugged and wiped my tail on the grass to re-move the last of the paint. "But her money's not."

"Ah," said Natalie.

"Nicely put. So...will you humor our loony client and tail this ringtail?"

She saluted. "Aye aye, private eye."

I waved her off. "*Ay-yi-yi,* birdie."

The last minutes of recess were dribbling out like drool from a baby bobcat at feeding time. Even if my client was nuts, I figured I should spend those min-utes working the case.

Since I'd blown my cover with T-Bone's bunny friend, I decided to try squeezing something out of the mole with the tutu. (Not squeeze her with a tutu, squeeze her for information...ah, you know what I mean.)

Luck was with me. I spotted the ballet-loving beastie digging a hole behind the cafeteria. As I drew near, I flipped up the brim of my hat, donned some fake glasses, and whipped out a notepad.

Chet Gecko, Master of Disguise.

"Nice hole," I said in a nasal voice.

The mole started. She edged away from her hole and squinted up at me with eyes like two raisins sinking in a furry pudding.

"*Hnorf,* thanks," she said through a snout that looked like a handful of earthworms playing Twister. "It's what I, *hnorf,* do."

"Uh, yeah. What's your name?"

"Sarah Tonin. What's yours?"

I grinned insincerely. "Um, Ace Grabonowitz . . . from the school paper? We're doing profiles of out-standing sixth graders, and—"

"Are you an, *hnorf,* artist?" she said, smoothing her tutu with muddy forepaws.

"Um, no. A reporter."

She giggled. "Then how you gonna, *hnorf-hnorf,* draw my profile?"

"Oh, hee hee. I get it." My acting surprised even me. "Not that kind of profile—a story."

"Oh."

I raised pencil to pad. "It's on T-Bone LaLouche. You know him, right?"

Sarah brushed dirt from her paws. "T-Bone is

one of the, *hnorf,* coolest guys I know. I mean, he, *hnorf,* plays drums well enough to be one of the Stench Bombs, and—"

" *'Stench Bombs'?* "

"Yeah, the sixth-grade rock group. *Hnorf,* what kind of reporter are you?"

"Huh? Oh, the tone-deaf kind," I said. "Tell me more about T-Bone."

Her raisin eyes twinkled. "*Hnorf-hnorf,* well, he's cute . . ."

Ugh. Leave it to a girl to get right into the mushy stuff. But this time, the mushy stuff was just what I needed.

I scribbled on the pad. "Uh-huh," I said. "And does he have lots of girlfriends?"

Sarah giggled again. Her giggle was lousy with *hnorf*s. "Silly," she said. "Of course he does."

"Like who?"

"Well, there's—"

R-r-r-rring! went the bell.

The mole looked past me and frowned. "Oops," she said. "See ya later." Sarah headed off.

I glanced where she'd been looking but saw only kids bound for class. Dogging her footsteps, I said, "Hey! T-Bone's girlfriends?"

"Um, I don't know if I, *hnorf,* should be talking about this."

"Why not? Is one of those girlfriends . . . you?"
Her fleshy snout swung my way.

I watched for a telltale blush. Then I realized: How ya gonna spot a blush on someone with face fur thicker than a shag carpet?

"He's *not* my boyfriend," she said. "Look, you should, *hnorf,* talk to Oliver or Trixie. I gotta go."

Sarah chugged off, her pink tutu quivering with each step.

I watched her leave. This mole had more than earthworms on her mind. Still, a tip was a tip. I resolved to check out the slim lead she'd given me.

But first I had to chase down another slim lead: my passing grade in English.

3

The Blaming of the Shrew

Anne Gwish put the *koo* in *cuckoo*. Even
though she was a parakeet. Despite my better judg-
ment, she was my client. And despite my best efforts, she cornered me by the swings at lunchtime.

"What?!" she squawked. "You let T-Bone *see*
you? How on *earth* can you tail him now?"

"Well, I—"

Anne hopped from foot to foot, waving her
wings. "Of all the sloppy, smart-mouthed, jelly-
bellied—"

"You forgot 'lazy.'"

"Why, you can't even follow my boyfriend without getting spotted."

I pointed at her. "Your 'boyfriend' claims he
doesn't even know you."

She blinked. "And you didn't see through that? What kind of detective are you, anyway?"

A dumb one, for taking this case, I thought. Through clenched jaws, I said, "Don't worry—"

"*'Don't worry'?!*" Anne screeched. "Now I'll *never* know the truth about T-Bone." She started plucking out her feathers.

I held out my palms. "My partner, Natalie, is shadowing T-Bone now, and when we know something, you'll be the first to know."

The parakeet sneered. "Oh, like that makes sense," she said. "How can *I* be the first to know if *you* already know it?"

I sucked in a deep breath. Mom always said to count to ten when I got steamed, but with this dizzy dame, it might take a hundred. (And math has never been my strong point.)

"Chet! Chet!" My partner's voice was as welcome as a jumbo cricket Slurpee after a ten-day trek around the sun.

Natalie flapped pell-mell across the playground, straight toward us.

"Ah, there she is now," I said to Anne. "Relax. Everything is swell."

Natalie skidded to a landing. "Oh, Chet—something awful!" She panted.

"I knew it," snapped Anne Gwish, giving me a sharp, I-told-you-so look.

I ignored her. "Natalie, you remember our *client,* Anne," I said, hoping my partner would take the hint and cool it in front of our customer.

She didn't. "The worst thing has happened. You'll never believe—" she said.

"They canceled *Samurai Jackal*?"

"No, it's—"

"There's a worldwide chocolate shortage?"

"No, I—"

"You're in love with Placebo Domingo?"

"No!"

I gave up. "What?"

"I'm suspended from school!"

"Huh? You don't have to go to school?" I scratched my head. "I thought you said it was something awful."

"It *is,*" Natalie moaned.

She was serious. The crazy mockingbird actually enjoyed schoolwork.

Anne Gwish pecked my arm. "She's *suspended*?" said the parakeet. "What kind of—"

I brushed her off. "Button up, you," I said, and turned back to Natalie. "Hey, it's not so bad. You'll be a soap-opera queen, just like your mom."

"Chet, it's not funny. I can't come to school. They won't even let me work on cases with you."

"What?" I rocked back on my tail. "You're right,

that's not funny. How could they suspend you? You're Miss Straight-A's-for-Days."

"That's *Ms.* Straight-A's-for-Days," she said. "And Vice Principal Shrewer accused me of blackmail."

I stared, mouth gaping. This made about as much sense as my bogus science report on the sand dolphins of the Kalahari Desert.

"Blackmail?" I said.

Anne butted her green head into my shoulder. "She's a *blackmailer*?"

I butted back. "Park it and lock it, cheese-beak."

Tears trembled in Natalie's eyes. Her chin quivered. "Chet, I didn't do it."

"Of course not," I said. "But why does Ms. Shrewer think you did?"

"Well, I was tailing T-Bone, and I dunno... maybe he spotted me..."

"He—*mmf!*" Anne tried to interrupt, but a firm hand around her beak put a stop to that.

Natalie hopped in agitation. "T-Bone dropped a letter outside the vice principal's door. Ms. Shrewer caught me picking it up, and then she—"

"Aha! There's the blackmailer," a tight voice snapped. It was the no-nonsense shrew herself, Vice Principal Shrewer, with Principal Zero close behind her. "Come along, missy," she said. "I want you off this campus *now.*"

Both of them clamped a paw onto Natalie's shoulder and started to lead her away. Natalie twisted to look back at me.

"You've got to clear my name, Chet. Hurry!"

Ms. Shrewer spun my partner's head to the front. And just like that, they marched her off.

"*Mmf! Mgmng mf!*"

What was that sound? A mutant mink with a speech impediment?

Turning, I found that my hand still gripped Anne's beak. I released it.

"And what've you got to say for yourself?" I said. "What's so important that it couldn't wait until after my partner got kicked out of school?"

"You," she hissed, "are fired."

I shook my head. Where had I heard that one before?

4

You've Got Blackmail

My mind spun like a giddy preschooler. I felt like I'd fallen into Bizarro World, where up was down, black was white, and big sisters want nothing more than your complete happiness.

Natalie suspended? I was the one voted Most Likely to Be Booted Out of Fourth Grade.

I left Anne Gwish listing my faults and wandered the playground like a homeless homing pigeon. Students frolicked all around me. I didn't notice.

Why would Vice Principal Shrewer accuse Natalie of blackmail?

I stumbled, unseeing, through a dodgeball game. Kids shouted, but I kept puzzling.

Okay, Ms. Shrewer saw my partner with some

letter. But it was a long leap from there to blackmail. Unless . . .

Two things hit me at once: a realization and—

Whump!

A dodgeball. I sprawled forward. Hands and knees on the rough asphalt, I stared ahead.

Of course! Someone—probably T-Bone—was blackmailing Ms. Shrewer, and the vice principal had mistaken Natalie for the culprit.

I could fix these crossed wires by doing one simple thing: explaining matters to the school's head cheese, so he'd cancel my partner's suspension.

"We're tryin' to play here," said a skunk. "You mind moving?"

Okay, two simple things.

With a jaunty step, I waltzed through the doors of the admin building. Principal Zero would understand. After all, he might be tough, but he was fair.

His secretary, Maggie Crow, munched a take-out lunch at her desk. I looked it over: a millipede-and-garden-snail salad.

"Lean cuisine?" I asked.

The black bird eyed me over her slanted glasses. "I'm watching my girlish figure," she rasped. "Whaddaya want? You didn't come here to trade diet tips."

Behind the counter, a gleaming steel contraption stamped papers.

"What's that?" I asked. "Another spanking machine?"

Mrs. Crow slurped a millipede. "Even better—a report card robot."

"*Bzzz* . . . fail!" said the machine as it stamped another sheet.

I shuddered, thinking of my own report card. But then I bucked up. "I'm here to see your boss."

Mrs. Crow waved a wing toward the principal's door. "Who's stopping ya?"

Principal Zero was a massive tomcat with all the charm and manners of Genghis Khan on a bad day. He sat behind a broad black desk, licking the remains of a tuna-fish sandwich from his paws.

I eyeballed his desktop. A purchase order for the *Encyclopedia Kittenica,* stacks of report cards, an autographed photo of Bigfoot (signed, "From one party animal to another"), the latest issue of *Catsmopolitan,* and a desk calendar.

I read his calendar upside down. Tomorrow's entry said: "Lunch meeting w/M. Crow and Superintendent." These are the benefits of being able to climb on the ceiling—you learn to read upside down.

"Got a minute?" I asked.

"For you?" he rumbled. "No."

"Come on, boss man . . ."

"If it's about Natalie Attired, you can save your breath."

I stepped forward. "But she's—"

"Innocent?" he growled. "Sure. They all are. Everyone thinks you kids are a bunch of blameless angels. But *I* know what kind of trouble you're really up to."

"You don't understand," I said, planting my hands on his desk and leaning forward. "I know her; Natalie would never blackmail anybody."

Principal Zero looked at my hands. I took them off his desk.

"No, Gecko, *you* don't understand. I'm not taking the word of some snoop over my vice principal."

"But—"

His claws flashed out and dug into the scarred desktop. "Ms. Shrewer doesn't lie," he growled. "If you can *prove* she made a mistake, maybe we'll talk. Until then . . ." His heavy-lidded eyes cut toward the door.

"Take a hike?" I guessed.

"All the way to Kathmandu. Now bug off!"

I bugged. Never one to take defeat lying down (I prefer a comfy armchair), I headed straight for the vice principal's office. In for a dime, in for a dollar.

Ms. Shrewer sat talking on the phone, her back to me. I studied the shrew.

Her fuzzy, bullet-shaped head rose from the neck of a dress that was last in style around the time of the Spanish Inquisition. Two ears burrowed into the head as if trying to escape her voice, a voice that sounded like a twenty-foot blackboard being dragged across a roomful of claws.

I wished them luck. Ms. Shrewer had a poison tongue. Literally. If a shrew ever hocks a loogey at you, look out.

"'No'? You'll have to do better than that," she half whined, half snarled into the mouthpiece. "Keep looking!" The vice principal banged the phone down. Then, half turning, she plucked a piece of paper from her desk.

"Ms. Shrewer?" I said.

"Eh?" She flinched, shoved the paper into an open desk drawer, and spun to face me. "What do you want?"

"World peace, a monthlong vacation, and a triple-decker beetle-larva sandwich," I said. "But I'll settle for justice."

The shrew's tiny eyes narrowed. She threw a halfhearted smile on her face. "I'm afraid I don't understand."

Playing Mr. Reasonable, I plopped into her visi-

tor chair. "Me, neither. I know my partner's not a blackmailer, you know?"

"No..."

"And I know if *you* knew her like I know her, you'd know she wasn't a blackmailer, too." I spread my hands. "So now you know."

"No, no." Her smile dropped so fast it nearly singed the carpet. "You're talking," she snarled, "about Miss Attired."

"Bingo," I said. "Now, why do you think she was blackmailing you?"

Ms. Shrewer slammed her desk drawer. "That's private." She marched around her desk. "As in, *keep your nose out of my private business.*"

"I'm a private *eye*," I said. "As in, *I* can keep a secret."

"Not mine."

I leaned forward. "Someone else is blackmailing you. I'll find out who—no charge."

The shrew grabbed my shoulders and set me on my feet. "Get . . . out."

"I'm going," I said, walking to the doorway. "But I'm not finished. I'll prove Natalie's innocence if it's the last thing I do."

Ms. Shrewer pushed her pointy snout close to mine. Her breath reeked of fungus and grasshopper guts. "Mister," she hissed, "if you go poking around in my affairs, it *will* be the last thing you do."

"Aw, shucks," I said. "Does this mean I'm off your Christmas list?"

And—*bam!*—just like that, she slammed the door in my face.

Did I leave? Hey, even the world's worst actor recognizes an exit cue when he hears one.

5

Owl Play

First Mr. Zero shot me down, and then Ms. Shrewer clammed up. Two strikes. For Natalie's sake, I couldn't afford a third.

I wondered about the paper Vice Principal Shrewer had shoved into her drawer. Could it be the blackmail note? Or just an invitation to join the National Crabbiness Coalition?

Bright sunshine made me squint as I stepped outside. Sneaking into Shrewer's office would take some planning. But in the meantime, I could check out the low-down, stinking blackmailer himself: T-Bone LaLouche.

My feet led me to the edge of the sixth graders' playground. Lunchtime might have been three-quarters over, but call me an optimist: I saw it as one-quarter full.

What had T-Bone's mole friend said? Ask Oliver or Trixie? I slipped on glasses, flipped up my hat brim, and approached the teacher on yard duty.

"Hiya, chief," I said to the beefy bobcat. "Know any kids named Oliver or Trixie?"

He scowled down at me. "Who wants to know?" he said.

"Uh, Ace Grabonowitz, star reporter. I'm on a story."

The bobcat looked me up and down with suspicion. "Right," he said at last. "You'll find Oliver Suddon in that tree . . . detective."

Dang. My disguise skills needed some work.

Oliver Suddon was a plump screech owl with a face as memorable as the last word problem on a twelve-page math test. Everything about him screamed Industrial-Strength Nerd—from his Coke-bottle glasses to the pocket protector on his vest. His mild eyes were big as dinner plates. His feathers were brown as boredom.

As I stepped around the tree, Oliver's head rotated to watch me.

Ugh. I hate when owls do that.

"Howdy, sport, I'm—"

"Ooh! Ooh! Don't tell me," he said. "You're that detective lizard."

I stowed the glasses and fixed my hat. So much for *that* disguise. "Chet's the name; mystery's the game," I said.

"Wow. I've heard about you. Are you on a case?"

"Um, yeah, as a matter of fact."

Oliver flapped his wings in excitement. "Wicked cool!" he hooted. "You're gonna interview me? Ooh! Ooh! I can't wait to tell my friends."

His enthusiasm was touching. I know *I'd* be excited if I interviewed me. *Hmm*...that might be worth doing. I made a mental note to try it later.

"Just wanted to ask you about T-Bone LaLouche," I said. "For background." I leaned on the tree.

"Golly," he said, shifting on his branch. "Go right ahead."

"First, do you know if T-Bone has any particular enemies?"

Oliver frowned. "No...he's a cool guy. Everyone likes T-Bone."

I scratched my chin. "Okay, what about bad company? You know, friends that might get him in trouble?"

"Ooh! Ooh! You mean like the Stench Bombs?" he said. "He really wants to join the band."

My tail twitched. The Stench Bombs again? *Interesting.*

"Is that so?" I asked.

"Yes." Oliver pouted. "Lately, T-Bone's been spending more time with them and less time with our study group."

"And you think they're a bad influence?"

"Definitely!" said the screech owl. "He's not studying as much."

Anything that took *me* away from studying was a *good* influence. But I didn't mention that to Oliver Suddon, Dweebmaster of the Universe.

"Thanks, flappy," I said. "You've been a big help."

"Ooh, keen-o! Anything else I can do?"

I smirked. "Yeah, buddy boy. Point me to a girl named Trixie."

His feathered noggin spun on its shoulders again as Oliver scanned the playground. *Yuck.* I could never be an owl—too many trips to the chiropractor.

"There," he said, "in the lavender scarf. Trixie's in our study group, too."

"Ain't that just the bee's knees," I said. I strolled over to the bunny he'd fingered. Oliver flew off—to tell his friends he'd met me, no doubt.

Ah, fame. It's the burden we hotshot private eyes have to bear.

From the back, Trixie looked just like any rabbit. Long ears, cotton tail. The usual bunny thing. But when I tapped her shoulder, I got a surprise.

Trixie was Miss Fluffy—T-Bone's chum at my morning mishap.

"Oh, it's you!" she said, chuckling. Trixie turned to her seagull friend. "Kylie, it's the guy who fell off the wall! Remember, I told you?"

The seagull squawked. "Whatsamatter, Gecko?" she said. "Did your feet run out of stickum?"

I checked my finger pads. "*Eew*. It's not stickum . . ."

"It's not?" said Kylie.

"Yes, it's snot," I said, "and it's yours. Use a tissue next time."

The gull's beak shut with a snap.

I snagged Trixie's elbow. "Could I talk to you for a minute?"

The rabbit raised an eyebrow. "Well, all right. If you're not going to fall down on me again."

I led her away from Kylie the seagull. "It's about T-Bone," I said. "He's . . . mixed up in this case I'm investigating."

"Is T-Bone in trouble?" asked Trixie, clasping her paws.

"Could be," I said. "That's what I'm trying to find out. Have you noticed anything odd about him lately?"

"Like what?"

"Has he been sneaky, or in a bad mood? Does T-Bone have any problems with the school staff?"

"He—" Trixie glanced past me. "Maybe you should ask him yourself."

"Why? Has the big bullyboy threatened you?"

"No," said the rabbit. "But he's standing right behind you."

Ah. That explained the smell.

6

'Dillo Talk

I turned and looked up into the snarling face of T-Bone LaLouche.

The ringtail's lean chest puffed out, and two buff armadillos leered over his shoulders like gargoyle bodyguards. A trio of troublemakers.

"What's the big idea, Gecko?" he growled. "Why you sniffin' around me?"

"Actually, I'm trying *not* to sniff," I said, "in case you drop another stink bomb."

T-Bone sneered. "I don't like your face, Gecko."

"No one does. I get a lot of complaints, but it doesn't seem to get any handsomer."

His black eyes sizzled and his paws clenched into fists. "Beat it, chump. And stop talking trash about me."

I dug in my heels. "What trash?"

"Word on the playground is, you think I'm a blackmailer."

"Yeah?" I said. "Well, the playground lies."

His eyebrows puckered. "Sure. It lies beneath us."

"No, not lies, *lies*."

"Exactly," he said, and pointed down. "It lies right there. What's the big deal?"

"Never mind." I shook my head to clear it. "Um, anyhow, I don't think you're a blackmailer."

"You don't?"

"I *know* you're a blackmailer."

"You shut your yap," he snapped. T-Bone asked the armadillos, "Hey, guys, what do we do to lyin' lizards?"

"We bung up their boozle!" said the beefier armadillo.

"What's a *boozle*?" said the second one.

"Aw, you know . . . ," said Beefy 'Dillo.

"Their schnozzola?" said Number-Two 'Dillo.

"Naw," said Beefy.

"Their noggin?" asked T-Bone.

"Unh-uh," said the big guy.

"You mean, you bash their faces in?" I asked.

The trio turned to me. "Yeah, that's it," said Beefy 'Dillo with a smile.

Me and my big mouth.

The three toughs closed in like a shark's jaws on a scuba-diving dentist.

I stepped back. "You framed my partner. But you won't get away with it."

"Big talk, little gecko," sneered Number-Two 'Dillo.

"Grab 'im!" cried T-Bone.

I streaked across the playground with the three mooks hot on my tail. If only I could reach a building, I could scuttle up to safety. A sixth-grade classroom loomed just ahead.

"Yaaah!" And suddenly, so did the ringtail.

Blocked, I wheeled back onto open ground. But I was losing steam. Lunch sloshed in my stomach. My legs felt like lasagna noodles.

R-r-r-ring!

The class bell never sounded so good.

T-Bone and his buddies gave up when their teacher called. Panting like a spaniel in the Sahara, I trudged back to class.

I had escaped cruel and sadistic torture that would've maimed me for life.

Mr. Ratnose greeted us with a cheery, "Pop quiz, everyone!"

Or had I?

———

Recess found me frazzled and frustrated under the scrofulous tree. I racked my brains but still couldn't get a handle on the case.

On the one hand, T-Bone said he wasn't the blackmailer, but a real blackmailer could easily tell a lie.

On the other hand, I didn't know that his note actually threatened blackmail. It could've been a love letter to Ms. Shrewer. (Then again, maybe not.)

And on the third hand, T-Bone had come on strong for an innocent guy with nothing to hide....

Hmm. I didn't have three hands. I didn't have a clear head. I needed Natalie's brainpower. Maybe I could—

"*Hur, hur.* Hey, Chet!"

It was my classmate, Waldo the furball. Waldo was a...well...no one knew exactly what. He wasn't a monkey, he wasn't a mouse, he wasn't a woolly mammoth. He was just...hairy.

"Make it snappy, Waldo. I'm a busy lizard."

He grinned. "Okeydokey. I heard about Natalie. With your partner gone, you need a replacement. And here I am! *Hur, hur.*"

My cheeks got hot. I jumped up. "Natalie's not gone," I said, "just suspended. And I'm *not* replacing her."

Waldo held up his furry paws. "Alrighty," he said. "But please just let me help a little? I've always wanted to be a detective."

"Nothing doing."

He dug in his book bag. "Pleeease? I'll give you all my Roaches Pieces." The furball held out two bags of candy.

My stomach said yes before my brain could object. "Okay," I said, snatching the treats. "But just one assignment."

Waldo jumped up and down, showering me with long hairs. "Yippedy skippedy!" he cried. "When do I start?"

"Tomorrow. And Waldo?"

"Yur?"

"Keep it under your hat."

He glanced both ways, then nodded. "Gotcha, Chet. Top secret." And with that, Waldo tiptoed away from me.

I rolled my eyes. These junior detectives.

I grabbed the candy and scarfed half of it. With the sugar rush came an idea. It was time to do a little spying on the Stench Bombs. And just my luck, they were rehearsing in the cafeteria.

As I neared the building, the unmistakable strains of a hardworking rock band filled the air. Ah, the harmonies! And, oh, the rhythms! It sounded like a pack of weasels murdering an accordion with a sledgehammer.

Before I reached the door, someone tapped my shoulder. I spun, half expecting T-Bone. Instead I found Maureen DeBree, head custodian—a neat-freak mongoose with a thing for Mr. Clean.

"Hey, private eyeball," she shouted over the noise, "you got time for one case?"

"Only if it's a case of cricket pops," I yelled back. "I'm busy."

"You're *dizzy*?" she said.

I cupped a hand by my mouth. "*Busy!* I gotta help Natalie."

"Help *batteries*?" said the mongoose. "But thass why I like hire you. Someone's stealing batteries from the storeroom."

I shook my head. "No can do. Gotta help my partner first."

Ms. DeBree frowned. "You got the *farter's curse*?" she shouted. "Why you never say so? I catch you later." And with that, she pinched her nose and took off running.

Good custodian, bad hearing.

I wished I could've taken her case. My piggy bank was emptier than a skeleton's lunch box—especially since Anne Gwish fired me.

But I swore I wouldn't even look at another case

until Natalie was back at school with her name cleared.

That's true friendship for you. Or true stubbornness. Sometimes they're hard to tell apart.

7

Bomb Before the Storm

Fingers in my ears, I pushed through the wide cafeteria doors. The music slammed against me like a body block from an electric eel.

Onstage, two birds, a kingfisher and a crow, were torturing electric guitars. A burly raccoon thrashed the drums, while a ferret wailed into a microphone:

> *"No more teachers!*
> *No more books!*
> *That's for morons,*
> *Feebs, and schnooks!"*

Then they all screamed, *"School is for fools!"* about ninety-seven times.

It wasn't Mozart, but it got the point across.

A pack of groupies pressed against the stage. The girls squealed and made goo-goo eyes, and the boys ping-ponged into one another.

Ambling closer, I skirted the fans. I hoped the sight of a star detective wouldn't distract them and alert the Stench Bombs. Fame gets in the way of my sleuthing sometimes.

Just then, several dancers exploded from the pack and banged into me from both sides. *Bimmo! Bammo!*

Like a pinball possessed, I ricocheted off a rabbit, sideswiped a salamander, and crashed—*whonk!*—into a big fat cat.

"*Oof!*" I dropped like a steel-winged bumblebee.

The cat bent down and helped me up. "Say, don't I know you?" he shouted.

"Yes," I said modestly, "I'm that private eye you've—"

"Nah. You're the goofy lizard that fell off that wall. Looks like you dance as good as you climb."

And with that, he rejoined the groupies in their frantic pogo-ing.

At last, the song ground to a halt with a sound like a rhino losing his lunch in a wind tunnel. The crow and raccoon stopped to sneer at their fans. The other two Stench Bombs pulled back by the curtains for a private confab.

I eavesdropped on them from a nearby water fountain.

"No one suspects. Right, Twang?" the kingfisher asked.

"Roger," said the ferret. She glanced my way.

I slurped water until my cheeks swelled like a bullfrog's. Something was definitely up with these two punks.

"If ya blow this deal for us," said the kingfisher, "ya know what's gonna happen?"

"Roger," said Twang the ferret.

"Stop calling me Roger!" the bird squawked. "My name's Lamar."

The ferret hung her head. "Okay, Lamar."

My belly was flooding like the lower decks of the *Titanic*. But I couldn't budge.

"Now," said Lamar, "what about the letter?"

My ears perked up. *The letter?*

The kingfisher ruffled his feathers. "Did you drop it yet?"

"Ro—er, yeah," said Twang. "I gave it to the girl. She passed it to T-Bo—"

"*Shhh!*" The kingfisher scanned the room, giving me a stare.

I slurped like a runaway vacuum cleaner. Water cascaded from my mouth like I was an Italian fountain of The Mighty Lizardi. I could foresee some major bathroom breaks during computer class.

Lamar hissed, "No names. Ya never know who's listening."

He was right. And this detective had listened enough. Enough to know that the Stench Bombs and T-Bone were cooking up some kind of blackmail scheme.

And it smelled worse than the sweat socks of a thousand angry wolverines. (Trust me on that—I once worked in the laundry at summer camp.)

8

The Hardest Partner

The class bell jangled, sounding positively peaceful after the Stench Bombs' last number. I eased out the cafeteria door and sauntered down the hall toward my classroom. Things were finally starting to fall my way.

What can you say about lessons? On the Fun-o-Meter, they rank somewhere between Chinese water torture and Grandma's bingo night. After suffering through enough of them, we escaped Mr. Ratnose's clutches and headed home.

In the halls, someone tugged at my sleeve. "Oh, Che-et."

A simpering chameleon walked beside me. Shirley Chameleon, to be exact. She was the cootie queen of the fourth grade, and that's all you need to know.

"Shirley."

"Um, the school dance is Friday," she said. "It's girls ask boys."

"I'll alert the news media."

"The, uh, Stench Bombs are playing."

"So?"

She turned the most interesting shade of flaming rose. "So I was wondering," she said, "if you'd go to the dance with me."

"Well, I gotta say . . . ," I said.

"Yes?"

"That all things considered, I'd rather floss with barbed wire."

I left Shirley and her pout behind. Just outside the school gate, a familiar feathered face waited.

"Natalie!" I cried.

"Heya, Chet." She tried on a smile. But it was tight around the edges and didn't fit right. Her fudge-brown eyes looked troubled.

"How's the easy life?" I asked.

"Pretty darn easy," she said with a forced chuckle. "I watched five hours of TV today. Wanna hear a new joke?"

"If I have no other choice."

Natalie joined me for the walk home. "Okay, um . . . knock, knock."

"Who's there?" I said.

"Repeat."

"Repeat who?"

"Okay," said Natalie. "Who, who, who, who, who . . ."

It was pretty weak, even for Natalie. She tried a cackle, but it came out more like a choke.

I pretended not to notice. "So, uh, sounds like you're having a peachy time."

"The peachiest." Natalie gave me a sidelong glance. "How's my case?"

"Well, I might get some help from Waldo," I began.

"Waldo?!" she said. "Chet, stop goofing around and clear my name."

I shrugged. "Well, it hasn't been as easy—"

Natalie grabbed my shoulders. "I'm gonna go nuts at home! I miss the pop quizzes, the teachers, the cafeteria food, the homework—everything."

She was already nuts. But she was my friend.

"Cool your jets, partner," I said. "Let's park our carcasses in my office, and I'll fill you in over snacks."

After ten minutes of chomping and chatting, we'd made a serious dent in the velvet-ant fudge bars. But the case was a little tougher to chew.

I wiped fudge from my cheek and summed it up. "So, it sounds like T-Bone and the Stench Bombs are in cahoots."

"But why are they blackmailing Ms. Shrewer?" said Natalie. "And why did they frame me? It just doesn't make sense."

I wondered whether there was room enough in my gut for another fudge bar. Only one way to find out.

"Maybe they, *mmf,* thought you were on to T-Bone's scheme?" I said, chomping into the creamy fudge.

"But then why wouldn't they frame you, too?"

"Got me, sister."

Natalie cocked her head. "You know what we need?"

"Some mantis milk to go with the fudge?"

"No, you cockroach muncher, we need a look at those blackmail letters. They could tell us why all this is happening."

I sat up. "Exactly what I was thinking."

Natalie paced. "We just have to figure out how we're gonna get into Vice Principal Shrewer's office."

"What do you mean 'we,' beak-face? If you set one foot on that campus during school hours, you're out for good."

"But I—"

"Nothing doing," I said. "I'll tackle this one on my own, and you'll stay off campus like a good little juvenile delinquent."

Natalie gave me a long look. "If you say so," she said at last.

"I do." Then I leaned forward. "Now you can help me solve something really important."

"Which is?"

"What's a better follow-up to fudge: cicada crisps or blister-beetle gum balls?"

9

Fast and Furry-ous

Ah, lunch! It's the killer-diller, the caterpillar's kimono, the candied cricket atop the sponge cake of life. Of course, aside from being the high point of my school day, lunch was also the perfect time to case Ms. Shrewer's office.

I bumped my tray along the cafeteria line, waiting to load up with greasy delights. My keen nose detected blowfly lasagna, spittlebug salad, and—could it be?—maple mosquito scones for dessert.

My turn came. I pushed forward. "Give me two scoops of—"

"*Bzzz,* may...Ihelpyou?" A robot in an apron stood holding a ladle.

"What the—" I stepped back.

"Don't worry, Chet, honey," said Mrs. Bagoong, head cafeteria lady. The hefty iguana patted the robot on its square head. "Meet my new assistant Ygor, courtesy of the sixth-grade science class."

I checked out the robot. It had green lights for eyes, two tubular arms, and a body like an industrial floor waxer built by left-handed chimps.

"Sure, it can cook and serve," I said, "but can it do my homework?"

Mrs. Bagoong smiled. "Just place your order and watch what happens."

"Give me *four* scoops of lasagna, Ygor," I said, winking.

With a click and a whir, the robot went into action. It neatly lifted two chunks onto my plate. "*Bzzz,* thank . . . youcomeagain," it droned.

"Hey, what about my other two scoops?" I said.

"Only . . . two, *bzzz,* percustomer."

"Clever little thing, isn't it?" said Mrs. Bagoong. She turned away. "Next?"

I stuck out my tongue at the robot. Technology is all well and good, but not when it interferes with the nutrition a growing gecko needs.

Three minutes later, I brushed the crumbs off my shirt and dropped my tray on the dirty stack. I no-

50

ticed that the robots were only handling the easy chores—serving food and collecting trays.

Maybe their union contract saved them from dishwashing. Lucky droids.

I hoofed it out the door. Time for some serious snooping.

Only one problem: I hadn't yet figured out how to lure Ms. Shrewer from her office. I stopped and stroked my chin. From my earlier peek at Mr. Zero's calendar, I knew he and Maggie Crow were at a meeting. If I could only—

"*Psst,* Chet," said a voice, "I can help." It was

my classmate Waldo the furball, sporting a broad-brimmed hat, black cape, and Groucho glasses.

"*Psst,* Waldo. You *need* help."

"*Hur, hur, hur,*" he chuckled. "Call me Agent Z."

"Huh?"

"Reporting for duty." He saluted.

"Oh, right. Um, hang on." Turning away, I chewed my lip. Without Waldo's monkey business, I'd soon think of a way to distract Ms. Shrewer.

Just then, an idea struck me—a ridiculous, hopeless, long shot of an idea. (Not much different from most of my ideas, I grant you.)

I grinned. "Waldo," I said, "how'd you like to create a diversion?"

A couple minutes later, Waldo stepped into the flow of students leaving the cafeteria. "Ladieees and jelly beans," he cried, "step right up for the world's greatest magic show!"

Kids being kids, most of them ignored him. But Waldo was used to being ignored.

He plucked out some firecrackers from his Big Bag o' Magic. "I call this trick The Exploding Furball. Don't be surprised if someone gets maimed for life!"

Now he had their attention.

I ambled toward the office, one ear cocked. Thirty seconds later, I heard it:

Ba-ta-KOOM! went the fireworks.

"Aieee!" went the kids.

Distraction, thy name is Waldo.

I raced down the hall and into the office. "Help, help!" I cried. "They're blowing up the cafeteria! Kids are getting hurt!"

As I suspected, only a parent volunteer and Ms. Shrewer were holding down the fort. The parent, a skinny sparrow mom, gasped.

Fireworks crackled.

Vice Principal Shrewer stuck her head out her office door. "What's all this fiddle-faddle?" she snapped.

"Fire! Cafeteria!" said the mom, flapping her wings. "Help!"

The shrew's round face soured like horsefly yogurt that's been left out overnight. "Call the janitor, you nitwit. I'll meet her there."

The vice principal bustled out the door. While the volunteer was on the phone, I nipped down the short hallway and into Ms. Shrewer's office.

A breeze from the open window billowed the lace curtains. Without Ms. Shrewer in it, the office was tidy, neat, and almost welcoming. But I wasn't there to report for *Office Beautiful* magazine.

I had only a minute or two at best. Time to work fast.

Making a beeline for the desk, I tugged on a drawer. Locked.

Dang. I checked the keyhole. Smaller than my tail tip.

"Lookin' fur somethin', podnuh?" drawled a voice straight from a two-bit Western on late-night TV.

I whirled. A gray bird in a cap and sunglasses leaned through the window. His frown froze me in my tracks.

"Me? I, uh, was just, uh, getting something for Ms. Shrewer."

The bird took off the cap and shades. "Need any help?" asked Natalie.

Relief washed through me. Alarm followed it.

"You featherbrain!" I said. "What if she catches you? We've only got a minute."

Natalie climbed through the window. "Then we'd better make it quick, huh?"

Rather than argue, I pointed her toward the desk. I took the filing cabinet. With a soft *snick,* the drawer slid open. The files were so organized it was scary.

"Got a death wish?" I said, flipping through folders. "'Cause Ms. Shrewer will kill you."

Natalie looked up from picking the desk drawer lock. "Better to die on a case than to die of boredom on the living room sofa," she said.

I couldn't argue with that. "Any luck?"

She pulled the drawer open and rummaged.

"Bills, notepads, erasers, an army of sharp pencils, and some pink, lacy garters," she said. "You?"

I flipped through the files, reading the tabs. "Let's see . . . Absences . . . Administrative Expenses . . . Bangles and Baubles . . . Bingo!"

"Found something?" asked Natalie.

"Yes, right behind the Bingo file. *Blackmail*." I removed the folder and opened it. Natalie crowded closer.

A handful of pages nestled inside. In black type straight from a computer printer, the first sheet read:

Shrewer:

Time for the third payment. Leave the cash in a bag in the scrofulous tree at sunset Thursday. No funny business, or everyone will know your little secret!!!
P.S. Don't forget the chocolate!!

"*Mmm,* chocolate," I said. "A blackmailer after my own heart."

Natalie pointed at the note. "Thursday?" she said. "But that's tonight."

"Say, you're pretty good. Tell me, what time is it when Mickey's big hand is on the two and his little hand is—"

I reached for another letter, but just then a sound

in the hall made my nerves jangle like the phones at a Save Summer Vacation telethon.

Footsteps!

And they were headed straight for Ms. Shrewer's office.

10

Shrewed Move

"Cheese it!" I hissed.

Natalie grabbed her disguise and hopped to the windowsill.

I stuffed the file back into the drawer, slammed it, and dived out the window.

Kee-RUNCH!

I landed hard in the skreezitz bushes. As quietly as possible, I tried to free myself from the thorns.

"Chet Gecko!" a voice behind me shrilled. "What are you doing out there?"

The poisonous tones of Vice Principal Shrewer.

"Uh, feeling bushed?" I said, glancing around for Natalie.

The shrew leaned on her windowsill. Her face

looked like a poster for National Rudeness Week. "That glib talk may work with your teacher," she snarled, "but it doesn't fool me."

Skritch, skritch, skritch. A new sound caught my attention.

It was Natalie, with cap and shades in place, raking the grass.

If looks could speak, mine would've said, *Beat it, you bubblehead!*

"You there, gardener," said Ms. Shrewer. "Was this student in my office?"

"No, ma'am," drawled Natalie in an accent as thick as the cheese on a deep-dish termite pizza. "This young'un's been a-bushwhackin' long as I been here."

Natalie's mockingbird voice talents could've fooled her own mom. But would her disguise hold?

The shrew frowned at my partner. "Don't I know you?"

Natalie gulped. The silence stretched like a giraffe's suspenders.

"Uh, she's—*he's* a new gardener," I said. "From, uh . . ."

"Tallahassee," said Natalie.

"Timbuktu," I said over her response.

"Where?" said Ms. Shrewer.

"Out of town," Natalie and I said together.

The bad-tempered shrew looked from one of us to the other. Then Ms. Shrewer nodded at the "gardener" and turned back to me.

"I've got my eye on you, mister," she said. "You're on final-jeopardy probation. If even a shred of evidence connects you with this blackmail scheme, out you go—just like your no-good, diddly-poo, mockingbird friend!"

"'*Diddl*'—" Natalie fumed.

I coughed loudly. "Uh, diddle . . . you say '*final-jeopardy*'?"

"Not another word!" barked the vice principal. I'd never heard a shrew bark before. (And I don't care to again.)

I shot Natalie a look. Muttering, she shouldered her rake and strolled onward. With a deep bow to Ms. Shrewer, I backed away, saluting.

"Not even a gesture," she called.

I could think of a few choice gestures, but my dad spanked me the last time I used one. Dignified as always, I beat my retreat.

Somehow, the school day lurched to an end, like a seasick water buffalo staggering to its bunk. (Or nest, or corral, or wherever water buffalo sleep. I forget.)

Homeward bound, I was turning things over in my mind.

"Hey, Chet," called Waldo the furball. He caught up to me. Half the fur had been singed off his face, and what was left was blacker than a warthog's nostril.

"Pretty cool diversion, huh?" he said.

"The coolest." Actually it would've been cooler if he'd kept Ms. Shrewer busy a bit longer. But beggars can't be choosers.

"So . . . got any other assignments?"

"Yeah." I kept walking. "Your homework."

The furball frowned. Then his face cleared. Waldo looked around at the other kids walking past us toward the school gate.

"Oh, I get it," he said with a broad wink. "Go do my *homework*. Riiight, Chet, *hur, hur, hur.*" He whispered, "What's *homework* a code word for?"

"For doing the work that keeps you from flunking." I waved him off.

Just outside school property, I was passing a knotty pine tree when a figure leaned from its shadows and said, *"Psst."*

I turned. "Waldo, for the last ti—" The words froze in my throat.

"Howdy, Chet," said a familiar voice.

"Natalie!" I grabbed her shoulders. "Are you completely bonkers?"

"Well," she said, "I *am* your partner, so I've probably got a screw loose."

"Ha, ha." I steered Natalie down the sidewalk. "That was some dumb trick you pulled. She almost caught you."

Natalie shuddered. "Tell me about it. But, Chet, you don't know what it's like, staying home all day. I can't take much more."

"Well, suck it up, birdie," I said. "You've gotta let me handle this."

We walked in silence awhile, past kids and carpools and crossing guards. Finally, Natalie and I stopped in my driveway.

"So?" she said. "Shall we stake out the scrofulous tree at sunset?"

I folded my arms. "*We're* not doing anything. *I'm* handling this stakeout."

Natalie's eyes narrowed. "The heck you are," she said. "This is my suspension; I should be there."

"Dream on, birdie," I said, heading for my backyard office. "I go alone."

"We'll just see about that."

And an hour later, we did. Loaded with snacks, I headed back to school. With Natalie. Never underestimate the persuasive powers of a dame—especially one with the mouth of a mockingbird.

11

For Heaven's Stakeout

If you've never tried nesting under krangleberry bushes, I don't recommend it. The berries smell as sweet as a gorilla's armpits on a muggy day. And the leaves? Well, let's just say when you lie on them you learn what put the *krangle* in *krangleberry*.

Still, the bushes were the best place for us to stake out the scrofulous tree. Natalie and I wormed our way in under the low branches and settled down to wait.

At least we had snacks.

Long shadows stretched across the playground like elastic black mamba snakes. Sunset was close at hand.

I tore the wrapper off a pack of Earwig Newtons. "Cookie?" I asked.

Natalie shook her head and stuck her beak into a bag of Entrail Mix—a combo of bug guts and granola. Health food.

"So, who do you think will pick up the loot?" she asked. Natalie fiddled with the camera we'd brought to catch the blackmailers in action.

"My money's on T-Bone," I said around a mouthful of cookie.

"Yeah . . . ," she agreed, "but what's his motive for blackmail?"

"He wants to join the Stench Bombs?"

"Maybe. But that's a long way to stick your neck out, just to play rock and roll. I think the Stench Bombs will pick it up themselves."

I chewed on that awhile. "But why would the Stench Bombs be blackmailing Ms. Shrewer? Why do they need the moola?"

Natalie placed a wing tip on my forearm. "Chet, look!" she said. "It's the diddly-poo shrew herself."

I glanced up.

A compact shape marched across the playground, as relentless as the first day of school. The last rays of the sun cast her shadow before her like the carpet at a blockbuster movie premiere—only this carpet was as black as her mood.

Even at a distance, I could tell: This was one surly shrew.

Natalie and I pulled the branches lower, to hide our faces.

Ms. Shrewer trundled up to the scrofulous tree, only fifteen feet away. She scanned the area and stared up into the tree. Then she wrinkled her nose, sniffing the air.

"I hope you took a bath," Natalie muttered. "Shrews have sharp noses."

"But just because she smells well doesn't mean she smells *good*."

It wasn't *that* funny. Still, Natalie and I had to clamp our hands over our mouths to keep from busting up.

We made no noise, but the bushes quivered. Ms. Shrewer squinted in our direction. She sniffed again.

Natalie and I held our breath. I didn't dare look at her.

At last, the vice principal turned away and dug a paper bag from her purse. The shrew shinned a little ways up the tree, placing the bag in the lowest fork.

"I know you're out there," she called as she climbed down. "I'm leaving what you asked for, but if I ever find out who you are, your tush is mush and I'm the blender."

With a last glance at the bushes, Ms. Shrewer stomped away, growling.

I waited until she was beyond earshot. "Did you

catch that?" I said. "Sounds like she knows you aren't the blackmailer."

Natalie cocked her head. "Or maybe she thinks I've got an accomplice. You'd better watch your step."

"My step?"

"Yeah," she said. "Don't step out of line."

"But can I step up my investigation?"

"As long as you take it step-by-step."

"Ah, step off, birdie."

Darkness pooled on the playground. The sun disappeared. Twilight fell.

The shrew's figure vanished. Soon, a car engine gunned.

I slipped out from under the bushes, camera dangling.

"Chet, wait!" said Natalie.

"No way." I hotfooted it for the tree. "I wanna check the bag for clues before the blackmailers show up."

Natalie crept forward and stood searching the night. "I'm not sure that's a good idea."

I scaled the tree. Inside the paper bag lay five stacks of crisp bills and a Three Mosquitoes candy bar. I'd like to say my keen detective sense led me to check the bills first, but I'd be lying.

Even in the dictionary, *chocolate* comes before *investigation*.

I grabbed the bar, unwrapped it, and took a bite.

"Come on, Chet," said Natalie. "There's no time for—*shh!* What's that?"

I froze. Then I heard it: Soft voices in the gloom, drawing closer.

"Hide!" hissed Natalie. She dived back under the bushes.

Too late to jump—they'd spot me for sure. I dropped the rest of the candy in the bag and scrambled up the branch.

Footsteps crunched over leaves. "See anything?" said a rough voice.

"Nah . . . *choo*," said a higher voice, with a sneeze. "Too gloomy."

As long as I stayed mum, I was safe. *I'm glad it's dark,* I thought.

Just then—*click*—someone turned on a flashlight. *Oh, darn.*

12

Tree-for-All

The mysterious visitors shone the flashlight up into the fork of the tree, just below the branch I clung to. I held my breath. My tail curled.

"There's the bag," said the first voice. "Boom-chukka, grab it."

By the flashlight's gleam, I made out three punks below: The ferret, Twang; the kingfisher, Lamar; and the burly raccoon, Boomchukka. So the Stench Bombs *were* behind the blackmail scheme. But why?

The raccoon stretched for the bag and handed it down to Lamar. The bird barked out commands. "Twang, Boomchukka, search the area."

The ferret circled the tree, nose to the ground. Her pal pawed the bushes.

"So?" said Lamar.

"Well," she said. "I *think* we're alone."

"Ya *think*?" asked the kingfisher, shining the light on her.

"Ah-ah-*allergies!*" said Twang, with a sneeze. "Pollen stuffs up my sniffer."

Lamar waved a wing. "No prob. Let's check it out." The three mugs surrounded the sack, gloating. They were going to get away with it.

Not if I could help it. I grabbed the camera still dangling from my neck. Time for a Kodak moment.

The kingfisher pulled out a wad of cash and whistled. "Looky, looky." He tucked some bills into his T-shirt pocket and dropped the rest back in the bag.

"Lamar!" said Twang. "What if he misses it?"

"Don't be a worrywart." Lamar examined the candy bar. "Hey, someone's been into this. What's—"

I raised the camera. "Watch the birdie, birdie!"

The three Stench Bombs looked up.

Pah! The flash exploded light.

"It's the gecko!" said Boomchukka.

"You're dead meat, bub," said the kingfisher.

"No," I said. "You are."

Fzzzt! The Polaroid camera spit out the photo. I grabbed for it, fumbled, and down it fluttered.

The kingfisher caught the photo. "Nice shot," he said. "Get 'im, Boom!"

"Uh, is this fair, three against one?" the massive raccoon asked.

"Get 'im!"

"Oh, okay." Boomchukka dug in his claws and began climbing.

Yikes!

I leaped onto another limb and scrambled farther up. The flashlight followed me like an annoying little sister.

Leaves slapped my face, branches tore my hide. Then the camera strap snagged.

I tugged. Stuck.

Boomchukka climbed steadily. He stepped onto my limb. It swayed.

I tugged again, and the strap unsnarled. In a flurry, I climbed to the end of the branch. It dipped like a deranged tango dancer.

The raccoon shinnied out, closer and closer.

The limb creaked and bobbed like a fishing rod landing Moby Dick.

I was too far out to reach another branch. Only one thing could save me. "Natalie!" I cried.

Wings flapped in the darkness. "Going my way?" she said.

With legs wrapped around the swaying branch, I reached for her feet, missed, and grabbed again. This time I got my mitts on her.

"Fly!" I shouted.

Natalie flapped her wings madly.

Boomchukka's outstretched hand grazed my foot. "No faaiiiiir!" he cried, missing me and losing his grip.

A quick glance back showed a dark shape crashing down through branches and flattening two other shapes like a bomb—a Stench Bomb.

Whump!

The flashlight fell. Voices clamored.

Natalie's wings flailed, trying to carry the extra weight. We plummeted groundward. My stomach tried to climb into my throat, and my throat wasn't pleased with the company.

"Any chance you're ... starting ... a diet soon?" Natalie panted.

"No, but another dip like this and I'll ralph."

The ground zoomed up to meet us.

Luckily for the future of the detective biz, my mockingbird pal pulled out of the dive and set a course toward home.

I took another gander at the Stench Bombs. Their flashlight beam weaved, and shouts reached my ears. But we had a head start on the three goombahs.

Flap, flap, flap. Natalie's wings thrummed a ragged drumbeat.

As we cleared the bushes on the playground's

far side, a pointy-eared figure reared up out of the gloom.

"Hey!" shouted the creature.

"Look out!" I cried.

Natalie wheeled away. Her breath rasped like a sore-throated Santa croaking his last carol. When she flapped over the school fence, the wire scraped my tail.

"Watch it!" I said.

"This . . . is . . . far . . ."

Natalie dipped, my feet caught a trash can, and we belly flopped—*ka-thomp!*—onto someone's lawn.

"Enough?" I said.

I helped my partner stand, and we staggered along the street toward home. Good thing the Stench Bombs didn't follow us; we had as much pep as two fizzled firecrackers in a toilet bowl.

"Close call," said Natalie.

"No foolin'," I said. "We almost bit off more trouble than we could chew."

I turned up my driveway.

"But the trouble's not over yet," said Natalie.

"What do you mean?"

She looked up at the figure of a gecko in my doorway, hands on its hips. "Chet, did you bother to tell your mom you'd be late for dinner?"

13

Bright-Eyed, Ambush-y Tailed

The next day, sunrise sparkled with all the colors of a baboon's butt—lavender, violet, and crimson. Oblivious, I plodded to school. I wasn't depressed, exactly; it was just morning, the armpit of the day.

Thoughts rattled around in that rusty bucket of nuts and bolts I call my brain.

I knew who the blackmailers were—in fact, it seemed like a broad conspiracy between the Stench Bombs, T-Bone LaLouche, and the mysterious, pointy-eared watcher in the bushes.

Only problem was, I had no solid proof. If I told Principal Zero what I'd seen last night, it'd be the Stench Bombs' word against mine.

And I knew what kind of weight my word carried with the principal—about as much as a gnat's nostril hair in deep space.

I pushed my way between kids clogging up the sidewalk.

Two robots directed traffic at the crosswalk. "What's with the droids?" I asked a nearby sixth grader.

"It's our class project," she said. "Robots Lend a Helping Hand. They're working all over school."

"Huh. Whaddaya know?"

This was probably saving Mr. Zero a pretty penny in crossing-guard salaries.

But even that wouldn't put Big Fat Zero in a good mood.

As I stepped past a robot, it whirred and motored toward me. "Cross... withcare," it droned, running over my foot.

"Ow! Watch it, bucket-head!"

The robot's eyes gleamed. "Have a, *bzzz*... niceday."

I'd swear the thing was laughing at me. Crummy machine. It somehow dodged my kick, so I moved on.

With one eye peeled for Stench Bombs, I hustled to the library. Our librarian, Cool Beans, was one savvy possum when it came to the criminal and supernatural. Maybe he'd know how to stop these blackmailers.

I made it to the library steps. So far, so good. But as I started up them, a voice grated, "Ah-ah-ah. Hold it right there."

I whirled. A crow, a kingfisher, and a ferret stood before me. Three little Stench Bombs, all in a row.

"Well, well," I said, "if it isn't the Stenchy Chapter of the Chet Gecko Fan Club." I eased up a step. "If you want autographs, you'll have to wait in line."

"Smart mouth, Gecko," said Lamar.

"It's been to school." I took another step back and stretched out my hand for the door. "Say, aren't you missing a Bomb? Where's Boomchukka?"

The door swung open. A funky whiff of damp fur and B.O. washed over me.

"Uh, right here," said Boomchukka.

I ducked under his grab and sprang for the wall, scrambling up it as fast as I could scram. On the library roof, I faced them.

"Ha, ha, suckers!" I said. "Try to catch me now."

The kingfisher and crow flapped their wings and started after me.

Oops. Memo to self: Don't taunt enemies who can fly. I hightailed it across the roof and leaped down to the top of the covered walkway.

Lamar and the crow swooped overhead, just missing me.

"Get 'im, Fweeter!" squawked Lamar.

Before the two mugs could return, I doubled back, hopping onto the roof, dashing across it, and slipping down the building's backside.

"Where'd he go?" called Twang.

"Find him, ya yo-yos!" squawked the kingfisher.

Hugging the library wall, I crept along quietly. I peeked around the corner. The coast was clear.

Head down, I beat feet for the nearest building and—*fwhump!*—ran straight into something big, thick, and furry. Boomchukka?

Two paws gripped my shoulders and held me at arm's length. I looked up into the frown of that bobcat teacher I'd met on the sixth-grade playground.

"Easy does it," he growled. The cat, I noticed, had pointy ears, just like the silhouette of the mysterious blackmailer. "What's all this hullabaloo?"

I did my best to look like the model student I would never be. " *'Hullabaloo'?* Who?"

"You," he snarled.

"Ooh," I said.

"You're that detective who was pretending to be a reporter."

Twang and Boomchukka rounded the corner of the library, spotted us, and stopped dead.

"I, ah, was thinking about a career change," I said.

The teacher stared at the two Stench Bombs. His face was as hard to read as a Martian phone book.

After a pause, the ferret and raccoon nodded and wandered off.

The bobcat looked me over with ice-cube eyes. His paws tightened on my shoulders. "Better not play rough," he purred. "Someone could get hurt."

My snappy retort died unspoken. "Uh. Yeah."

His eyes narrowed.

The class bell pealed. *B-r-r-ring!*

And just like that, the iron paws relaxed. "Get to class, Gecko."

I trotted off. I hadn't been so glad to walk into Mr. Ratnose's room since the time Shirley brought a do-it-yourself sundae machine to science class.

The big bobcat had me sweating bullets. If he was one of the blackmailers, I had a feeling that this gecko was about to find himself in deep, deep doo-doo.

14

Trouble or Nothing

Come recess, I hotfooted it for the library like a millipede on a summer sidewalk. Without Natalie around, I needed the extra brainpower only our librarian could supply.

Inside, a passel of first graders swarmed over the long tables, giggling, pulling hair, picking their noses, and generally behaving in a dignified first-grade manner. My sister, Pinky, was among them.

I ignored her with the practiced calm of a big brother. Skirting the crowd, I made for the librarian's desk.

Two students ahead of me were checking out books, so I checked out the rest of the library. Other than the little kids, traffic was pretty light. A cluster of sixth graders were working at the computers. I looked closer.

Oliver Suddon, the owl, tapped on the keyboard while the mole Sarah Tonin and Trixie the rabbit watched over his shoulders. That must be Oliver's precious study group. But where was T-Bone?

"What's shakin', bacon?" said Cool Beans. The opossum librarian sat behind his desk, beret tilted jauntily on his massive skull, wraparound sunglasses reflecting the room. He was as cool as a polar bear's pantry.

"I'm working a case," I said, "and I could use your brain."

He grinned. "Copacetic, daddy-o. Just got it back from the cleaners."

Sometimes it doesn't pay to dig too deeply into a possum's personal life. I said, "This blackmail case has got me bamboozled. I think I know whodunit, but I can't get the goods on 'em."

Cool Beans leaned back and stroked his whiskers. "Who we talkin' 'bout?"

"T-Bone LaLouche, the Stench Bombs, and that bobcat teacher who's always in a bad mood."

"Kent Hoyt."

"What can't hoit?"

"No, no, *Kent Hoyt.* That's the cat's handle, his name."

"Oh," I said. "Anyway, looks like they're in this together, but I need proof."

"The proof is in the puddin'," he said.

My stomach rumbled. "I could use some pudding, too," I said. "But right now I'd settle for proof."

Cool Beans scratched his barrel chest. He scoped out the room slowly (like a possum does everything).

"Don't look now," he said, "but one of your suspects just made the scene."

I followed his gaze. That rotten ringtail, T-Bone, had joined his study group. Trixie and Sarah made way for him by the computer.

"I told you not to look," said Cool Beans. "Hey, Sherlock, want my advice?"

"Sure."

"Follow that old saying: When you rattle the door, the roaches will run."

I scratched my head. "So you're saying I should run with the roaches?"

The possum rolled his eyes. At least, I think he did—it was hard to tell behind those shades.

"No, man. I'm sayin' if you want the blackmailers to goof up, make 'em think you've got the drop on 'em."

"Ah." Not a bad idea. "Cool Beans, can I borrow some paper and a pen?"

The librarian snagged a flyer advertising tonight's school dance and flipped it over. "Will this do?" he asked.

With half an eye on T-Bone and half on my work, I scrawled a threatening letter.

Dear Mr. Blackmailer (and crew),
The jig is up. Your goose is cooked. I'm blowing the whistle on you today—right after school.
Say your prayers, pal.
—Mister E

When I finished the note, I folded it into an airplane. "Keep tabs on T-Bone for me," I said.

"Where you goin'?" said Cool Beans.

"To rattle the door."

I strolled back to the book stacks. At the edge, I turned, waiting for my chance. I glanced left, right, then hurled the airplane straight at T-Bone.

Before the missile hit, I ducked back out of sight.

"Che-et!" My little sister, Pinky, stood with hands on hips. "I'm telling."

"Keep it zipped, munchkin," I muttered.

"Nuh-unh," she said, getting louder. "I won't."

I gave her the Super Colossal Big Brother Death Ray stare. "You. *Will.*"

"Nuh-*unh*! You're not s'posed to throw—"

I clamped a hand over her mouth. Pinky struggled. "What'll it take to shut you up?" I hissed. "A custard maggot cup?"

Her eyes smoldered. Slowly, Pinky's hand came up, showing three fingers.

"*Three?* That's—oh, all right." I removed my hand. Pinky smiled. "Three a day," she said.

"Don't push it."

She stuck out her tongue at me and wandered back to join her class. If you ask me, little sisters are the mothballs in the milk shake of life.

I ambled back to Cool Beans's desk. Without looking at T-Bone, I asked the librarian, "Well? How did he react?"

"Hard to say," said Cool Beans.

"Why's that?"

"Your airplane wobbled, Wilbur."

"Where did it land?" I asked.

"Smack-dab in Oliver's lap," said the possum.

The class bell rang, cutting our talk short. As I strolled to the door, I glanced over at the computers.

Oliver's study group whispered with heads together. The last thing I saw on the way out was T-Bone's narrow mug watching me and scowling.

I'd lit the fuse. Now we'd see how this firecracker went kablooey. (And whether it would blow up in my face.)

15

Mum's the Bird

Lunchtime passed peacefully enough. Too peacefully. None of my suspects staged a kidnapping, stole a tank, or broke down and confessed.

Sometimes detective work can be harder than a week-old sowbug biscuit. (Which, coincidentally, is what they served with lunch.)

Back in Mr. Ratnose's class, I let my mind wander. (Not that I usually stopped it.) Questions circled like termites around a porch light.

Who was giving the Stench Bombs their orders? Would my note nudge the blackmailers into making a mistake? And would my parents break down and buy me a ticket to the wrestling rematch of "Spoiled Beef" Stroganoff and Antone "The Stone" Jones? (Hey, a gecko can dream, can't he?)

At the front of the class, Mr. Ratnose jabbered on. He claimed to be teaching science, but I knew the truth: It was a cruel experiment in Death by Boredom.

Ten minutes before recess, a lemming showed up at the door with a note. My teacher pointed the little rodent toward me.

"Note for you," he said.

"Who from?"

The lemming shrugged. "I dunno. Some bird janitor in sunglasses."

Natalie. I smiled and unfolded the note.

The messenger coughed. "No tip?" he said.

"You want a tip? Never order Chef's Surprise in the cafeteria."

The lemming sneered and shuffled off. I read the note.

Chet,
Important developments! Meet me at the scrofulous tree at recess.
N.

Ha! Good old Natalie—she'd discovered something.

I watched the clock. When the recess bell blared, I rocketed from my seat like a hoptoad with electrified underpants. In less time than it takes to forge a permission slip, I was standing beneath the scrofulous tree.

Other kids poured onto the playground. I watched closely. Would Natalie disguise herself as a substitute teacher next? A Ukrainian bug smuggler?

Minutes passed. No Natalie.

A pack of second graders played a spirited game of Chase Me Till I Conk Out. They giggled until their lunch almost made a reappearance.

After ten minutes, with recess slipping away, I sat down at the base of the tree. And that's when I saw it: a red, liquid smear on the ground.

I crouched and leaned over the puddle. Was it blood? I sniffed. Hard to tell.

It could've been just the jelly from a beetle-jelly sandwich. But I wasn't about to taste it to find out.

I tried to keep my chin up. But dark thoughts crowded my mind like a bully cutting into the lunch line.

Was Natalie hurt? Or worse, had she been murdered over what she knew?

One thing was for sure: When the class bell rang and she still hadn't shown up, I knew the reddish stain meant something bad.

When I returned to my desk, I found out what. A note greeted me. Scrawled in crude crayon, it read:

Gekko,
We got whut you want. Meet beehind the portabuls after shool.

I sagged into my seat. What had I started? The blackmailers had snatched my partner; they'd made their move, all right.

And I hoped they believed that a bird in the hand was worth more than one in the ground.

16

Put on a Happy Chase

The school day ended, not with a whisper but with a clang. (The clang of the bell, to be exact.) While my classmates rushed past, I stalked down the halls like little David on his way to the Goliath family reunion.

My neck and shoulders prickled. The showdown was at hand.

I skirted groups of gabbling girls. The school dance wouldn't start for a while, so students lounged around, killing time.

Not me. I was a lizard with a mission. Actually, two missions: rescuing my partner and busting the blackmailers.

By the time I reached the portables, they were

empty as Flunkenstein's brain at test time. I crept between the buildings.

What I needed right then was a brilliant plan, a couple of football teams as backup, and a black belt in kung fu. All I had was luck and pluck.

And my luck hadn't been all that great lately.

I peeked around a corner. In the building's shadow stood Lamar and Twang, two of the four musical thugs known as the Stench Bombs.

"Don't be shy, bright boy," said Lamar. "Join us."

"Gee, thanks," I said, drawing near, "but I don't play an instrument."

The kingfisher's laugh was as fake as my book report on Famous Popsicles of the Nineteenth Century. "Check out the comedian, Twang," he said. "Funny, eh?"

"Roger that," said Twang the ferret.

"Twang, what did I tell ya about calling me Roger?"

"Sorry, Lamar."

The bird turned back to me. "Listen, joke boy, we got something you want," rasped Lamar. "And if ya wanna see her again, ya gotta play ball."

I crossed my arms. "I was dodgeball champ, two years running. Let's play."

Lamar ruffled his feathers. "Last chance, smart mouth. Ya want your partner; we want something from ya."

"Yeah, what?"

"The goods."

"The goods?" I raised an eyebrow.

"The goods you got on us," said Twang.

"Oh," I said, "*those* goods."

The kingfisher took a step toward me. "So, whaddaya got?"

"The goods," I said.

"Yeah, and what *are* they?" the ferret snarled.

"Oh," I said, "they're good. They're really, really good."

Lamar and Twang exchanged a look. The kingfisher moved to my right, while his sidekick edged left. I stepped back.

"Come on, Gecko," Lamar squawked. "Spill the beans."

"All right," I said, "I know about your little blackmail scheme."

Lamar scoffed. *"Blackmail?* We were doing a pickup for a friend, and we took a tiny carrying charge. How is that blackmail?"

I backed up another step. A twig cracked behind me. I spun.

Boomchukka bulked, wide as the backside of a bulldozer. I darted between Twang and Lamar, and whirled to face the three lugs.

"Do I look like a balloon?" I said.

"Uh, no," said Boomchukka.

"Then stop filling me full of hot air."

"Okeydokey," said the kingfisher. "Take 'im, guys!"

"Uh, technically," said Boomchukka, "we're not all *guys*. I mean, Twang and Fweeter are girls."

Twang slunk forward. I backpedaled.

"Ya know what I mean!" snapped Lamar. "Get Gecko!"

Whirling, I made like a bakery truck and hauled buns. I aimed for the gap between two portables.

"Caw, caw!" Fweeter the crow dive-bombed from the roof, straight for me.

At the last second, I tripped and fell, *foomp!* (Not exactly the kind of move that'd win me a spot on the football team.)

Thomp! Two bodies collided just behind me—Twang and Fweeter, no doubt.

I hopped up. Vaulting a skreezitz bush, I fled down the hall, back toward the other classrooms. Maybe I could ditch the Stench Bombs or hide in the office.

If I could outrun them.

My heart thudded like Boomchukka's gnarliest

drum solo, and my breath grew shorter than a mite's stepladder.

Fwamp-fwamp-fwamp. Wings thrummed behind me.

I ducked, and Lamar's swoop grazed my hat. A corridor opened on the left. I took it, while the kingfisher rushed past.

With only seconds to hide, I scanned the building. Locked tight.

Then a puzzled face popped up beside a nearby bush.

"What's, *hnorf,* happening?" said Sarah Tonin, the mole. Her eyes widened. "Quick, down here!"

Sarah leaped from her hole. I dashed for it and plunged in headfirst.

Down, down, down in darkness I tumbled, bumping and sliding. The tunnel surface was slicker than a sixth grader's excuse note. At a sudden curve, light dazzled my eyes. I shot from the tunnel and landed—*boomf!*—

facedown in some kind of netting. Thoughtful touch, that.

"Intruder alert," a tinny voice blared.

Huh?

Then, with a click and a whir, three robots gathered the ends of the net.

"Nice and tidy," said a familiar voice. "Make sure it's tight."

"*Bzzz,* yesmaster," a robot droned.

I rolled over, blinking. Electric lights revealed a good-sized chamber. And standing in the center, his mild eyes framed by thick glasses, was the screech owl, Oliver Suddon.

"Wicked cool," he said. "Look who just dropped in."

17

Buy Low, Cell High

Ponk, *ponk, ponk.* My butt bumped the ground as the robots dragged me along a corridor. What was happening here? My brain raced like a four-year-old at bath time.

"Oliver?" I said.

"Mm?" he answered, strolling just ahead.

"If your pals got you into some scheme, and you want a way out, I can help."

Oliver's head swiveled. His dinner-plate eyes grew even wider. "Really?"

"Sure, I know how awful peer pressure can be," I said. "Just let me go, and I'll get Ms. Shrewer to take it easy on you."

The screech owl's face split in a grin. "Let you

go? Ho, ho, ho! Peer pressure—ha, ha, that's droll!"
His eyes twinkled. "You have no idea, do you?"

I forced a laugh. "Hah! Of course I do. I know exactly"—Oliver's contemptuous gaze met mine—"nothing about what's going on here."

"I thought so."

He faced front again. We kept walking (or in my case, bumping).

Oliver stayed quiet, but then, like a kindergartner with a juicy secret, he couldn't help talking.

"Ooh! Ooh! Here's the thing," he said, "*I'm* the one applying the pressure."

My jaw dropped. "*You're* the blackmailer?"

"'Blackmailer'?" He sighed. "And I thought you were such a hotshot detective. Don't you see my plans go far beyond mere blackmail?"

"Huh?" My interviewing technique was stellar. Usually.

Oliver led the way down a flight of earthen stairs. *Bimp, bamp, bomp!* The robots jounced me even harder. When I craned to look up at their square heads, I could've sworn they wore mechanical smiles.

"Blackmail is just how I finance my grand design," said the screech owl.

"But why?"

"Because allowance money can only stretch so far."

Our pathway leveled out. This part of the tunnel was muddier than the chamber above. I tried to memorize its twists and turns.

"So what's the expensive scheme?" I asked. "A trip to Bora-Bora? The complete set of Punky-Man trading cards?"

Oliver's steps slowed. "Oh, just a little thing I call Science Project Number Nine. Haven't you noticed my little creations around campus?"

Creations? Then it hit me—robots in the cafeteria, robots at the crosswalk, robots carting me around. I blinked. "You mean . . . ?"

"Yes," said Oliver, "I'm building a robot army to take over the school!"

"*This* school?" We entered another chamber, whose ceiling disappeared in shadows. "But why?" I asked again.

The owl turned to me and shrugged. "How else am I going to become the world's youngest evil genius? You gotta have a robot army—all the best criminal masterminds do."

I couldn't argue with his logic. (Since he was about as logical as a dodo bird dreaming of getting into Harvard.)

The three robots hooked my net to a huge mechanical claw. With great relish, Oliver fluttered to a control panel and punched some buttons.

A metal arm lifted the claw, hoisting me into the air. It swung me toward a blocked-off corner of the chamber and dangled me above it.

"Cool, huh?" he said. "I designed it myself, with some help from my study group." His voice grew ominous. "And now, Chet Gecko, prepare to meet..."

"My doom?" I said.

"You'll see," said Oliver.

And with that, the claw released a corner of the net. I dropped like an overripe papaya down into a metal holding cell.

A dark shape stirred. I tensed.

"Heya, PI," said Natalie. "Come here often?"

18

Fresh Sprints of Bel-Lair

Natalie huddled in a corner of the gloomy cell. I rushed to her.

"Partner!" I said. "When I saw that red goo by the tree, I thought you—"

"I know," said Natalie. "Oliver cracked my disguise, and he had the Stench Bombs snatch me."

I looked her over. "But are you hurt? I mean, the blood..."

She shook her head. "Red beetle jelly."

"*Dang.* I knew I should've tasted it."

Outside the metal box, Oliver chuckled. "I'll leave you to your tearful reunion," he said. "Chet and Natalie, sitting in a tree, K-I-S-S-I—"

"*Eew!*" said Natalie and I together.

"And now it's showtime," said Oliver. "The school dance will see a performance in a million. When we attack, *everyone* will be doing the robot."

"But won't that tick off your partners, the Stench Bombs?" I said.

"Those bozos? They're just pawns. Besides, they've got it coming; I saw them rip me off." Oliver's voice faded as he moved. "See you later, suckers."

And he was gone.

"So what was it you wanted to tell me?" I said.

"Huh?" said Natalie.

"That note you sent. What did you find out?"

Natalie spread a wing. "I found out where those missing batteries are going. You know, the ones you told me Maureen DeBree told you about?"

"You're telling me I told you she told me?" I shook my head. "That's not important now."

"Oh, yes it is," she said. "Oliver's using those batteries in his robots."

"Oh. So . . . what does that tell us?"

"It tells us we've gotta stop him," said Natalie.

"No duh," I said. "But how?"

I eyeballed the slick metal walls of our prison. Up, up they rose, to a—wait a second. The cell had no ceiling.

"Natalie, are these walls electrified?"

"Nope."

"Then how does he expect to keep us here?"

Our eyes met. "Let's go!" we said together.

I climbed, and Natalie flapped her wings. This was almost too easy. Our heads poked over the wall, and—*ba-POW!*—a padded beam batted us back into the cell faster than a teacher's pet at eraser-clapping time.

Yup, too easy.

"Ow." I picked myself up off the hard floor. "That Oliver and his inventions."

Tinny robot laughter echoed in the chamber. Steel-plated punks.

After a couple more tries, we had nothing to show for our efforts but bruises. The owl's machine was too quick for us.

"Okay," said Natalie, "I'm ready for Plan B."

I rubbed my sore head. "Me, too. Any ideas?"

Natalie paced. "Let's see . . . we could make a crude shovel with buttons, pocket lint, and the stub of a pencil, and then tunnel out of here."

I rapped my knuckles on the floor. "Solid steel." I sighed. "Too bad we can't just trick the robots. They seem about as bright as a box of rocks."

"Now that's an idea," said Natalie.

"Yeah, a dumb one. The robots only take orders from Oliver. To get them to obey, we'd have to . . ."

"Sound like Oliver? Wicked cool," said Natalie in the owl's nerdy voice.

You gotta hand it to those mockingbirds. They sure can mock.

"Go to it, partner," I said.

Natalie-as-Oliver called out, "You there, robots!"

"Yes, *bzzz,* master," droned three robot voices.

"Go to the control panel. Turn off the machine."

We heard a whirring as the robots obeyed, then a click. The chamber was plunged into darkness.

"Yup," I said. "Bright as a box of rocks."

After several more tries, Natalie got the three nut-and-bolt-heads to turn on the lights and turn off the guard machine. I scrambled up and over the wall, dropping to the muddy floor. Natalie glided down beside me.

The robots swiveled our way, their eyes changing from green to red.

"That doesn't look good," I said.

"*Bzzz,* intruder alert," said one robot.

Natalie did her Oliver impression. "No, no. These are friends; let them go."

"Must, *bzzz,* stopintruders," droned another robot. It blocked the door while the other two motored forward.

"Dang," I said. "Too bad you don't look more like him."

"What, and give up this pretty face?" said Natalie.

We retreated before the robots' advance until the cold metal wall pressed against our backs.

"Well," I said, "when talk fails . . ."

"Run like heck," said Natalie.

She flew up to perch on the cell's edge. I scaled the metal slab and jumped from it to the cavern wall.

"We're safe up here," I said. "At least those droids can't climb."

The two robots below gave a hollow chuckle. At the touch of a button on their arms, suction cups sprouted like zits after a pizza-eating session.

Thi-pock! Thi-pock!

They began climbing the wall.

"Yahhh!" Natalie and I cried. I jumped to the floor and darted for the entrance, with Natalie close behind. Together we rushed the doorway, bowling over the robot guard.

"This way!" said Natalie, flying down the corridor.

Her wing tips brushed the walls. I slipped and slid in the mud, trying to keep up. We charged through winding passages until my side ached.

"Whoa," I said, slowing down. "Let's walk. We got a head start."

"Really?" Natalie landed.

"Sure, I mean, how fast could those things possibly go?"

Just then, an alarm bell clanged. A mechanical

voice echoed in the tunnels: "Intruder alert! All-robots, *bzzz,* stopintruders!"

Natalie turned to look at me. "So, Mr. Robo-Expert, any other bright ideas?"

"Skedaddle!" I said.

We stumbled up a flight of steps and down a corridor. The tunnel narrowed. Natalie couldn't fly, so she ran with me. Then we hit a four-way intersection.

"Which path?" said Natalie.

I pointed left. "This one. I think."

"You *think*?"

We pounded down the passageway. From above came a muffled, rhythmic thumping.

"I'm almost sure this is it," I said.

Then we rounded a corner. I stopped short and Natalie skidded into me.

"Wha—?" Her question fizzled out.

Filling the corridor from wall to wall and stretching out of sight was a robot army. Each robot's eyes glowed red, and their voice boxes boomed one cry: "Crush, mush, destroy!"

And something told me they weren't talking about the recyclables.

19

Robo-Bop

Natalie and I cut and ran before the robot horde. When we returned to the intersection, robots filled two of the other passages. They advanced with a relentless whir, like a showroom full of vacuum cleaners gone berserk.

"*Rrrr!*" they cried.

"*Wahhh!*" we screamed.

Only one path lay open to us. We took it at top speed.

The tunnel broadened again as it rose. The thumping above boomed louder.

"I think we're almost out," said Natalie.

"Good," I said. "'Cause they're getting closer."

With the killer robots only yards behind us, we

rounded a corner and reached the tunnel's end. The dirt floor sloped up into the ceiling.

"A dead end?!" said Natalie.

"Unless you're part earthworm," I said.

But as we drew nearer, cracks showed in the ceiling. Light streaming through these cracks revealed a trapdoor.

"Push, Natalie!"

We put our backs to the panel and shoved.

The robots closed in.

For a heart-stopping moment, the door stuck.

Then it gave—*wham!* We tumbled out into an explosion of light and noise. Creatures writhed in agony to horrible sounds of destruction.

"We're too late!" I cried.

"No," said Natalie, "it's just the dance."

Then the scene snapped into focus. A punk-rock frenzy gripped the cafeteria. Music pounded, kids gyrated, lights flashed, and chaperones winced.

All this I glimpsed as we rolled away from the trapdoor and under the dancing feet. A chubby gopher nearly boogie-oogie-oogied onto my head. "Hey, watch it!" he said.

Natalie and I struggled to our feet, just as screams filled the cafeteria. The robots burst forth. Kids scuttled away from the trapdoor as if Godzilla himself had just passed gas.

"Aaieee!" Pandemonium broke loose.

I spotted Oliver by the hatch. "Get the grown-ups!" he shouted to his machine army. The robots pushed through the mob of squealing kids and headed for the fringes of the room, where teachers and parents tried to restore order.

Oddly enough, the Stench Bombs kept right on playing. Probably didn't want to waste all that practice.

"You! Gecko!" A green parakeet plowed through the crowd, straight at me. It was Anne Gwish, former client.

"I'm a little busy right now," I said. "Come back Monday."

She caught my arm. "No!" she squawked. "*You* let those awful robots in, and now they're wrecking my dance!"

"*Your* dance?" said Natalie.

"Of course," snapped Anne. "I organized it because it's my *destiny* to dance with T-Bone, and for him to be my *boyfriend*."

I shot a look at Natalie. She raised her eyebrows and circled a feather tip beside her head in the universal sign for *cuckoo*.

"The dance is falling apart," screeched the parakeet. "*Do* something!"

"Okay," I said. "How about the mambo?"

Anne Gwish gave an earsplitting *"Scree-ahh!"* and

flew at the nearest droid, knocking it into the re-freshment table. Mrs. Bagoong steadied the tubs of soup.

Just then, somebody slammed the cafeteria doors—*Clang! Clong!*—trapping us all inside.

"Chet, how do we stop the robots?" cried Natalie.

"Beats me," I said. "Sing 'Mr. Roboto'?"

She pulled me aside. "Think. They run on batteries . . ."

Fangs bared, Principal Zero rushed past us toward the robots. Some helmet-heads were going to
wish they hadn't tangled with that particular kitty.
Mr. Ratnose and Ms. Glick struggled with the waves
of evil machines pouring from the trapdoor.

"So how do we put the kibosh on their batteries?" I said.

Natalie gave me a blank look. "Dunno. We
haven't studied batteries yet."

"Me, neither." I scanned the mob scene. "Where's a science nerd when you need one?"

"Building a robot army?" said Natalie. She snagged my arm. "Come on!"

We elbowed our way into the free-for-all, ducking robot punches. When I saw her target, I said, "Wait, that's Kent Hoyt! He might be in on it."

Natalie shook her head. "No way. He's the new sixth-grade science teacher."

When we reached him, the bobcat was clonking two robots' heads together.

"Mr. Hoyt," I said, "how do you stop batteries from working?"

"This is—*unh!*—no time to discuss your science project," he said.

A third robot jumped onto his back and wrapped its arms around his throat.

"Please," said Natalie. "It's a matter of life and death."

"Try . . . salt water," he choked out. Then Mr. Hoyt doubled over, flipping the robot into one of its companions—*whump!*

We turned and shoved back through the crowd toward the kitchen.

"Salt water," I said. "Why didn't I think of that?"

"Because you got a C-minus in science?" said Natalie.

"There's that."

Natalie hopped to the kitchen door. "We'll find lots of salt back here."

"Wait a minute." I pointed at the tubs of soup on the refreshment tables. "There's nothing saltier than Mrs. Bagoong's wood-louse gumbo."

I leaped onto the table, dipped a bowl into the soup, and flung the brown goop onto the nearest robot. Its head turned and its red eyes flashed.

"Rrr!" The mechanical monster dropped first-grade teacher Mrs. Toaden like a full diaper. It rushed toward me, arms waving.

I hurdled over the table.

"Look out, Chet!" cried Natalie. "It doesn't like soup."

The droid chugged forward like a demented freight train.

20

Salt, With a Deadly Weapon

The robot bore down on me like Doom in a Bucket. Its eyes gleamed and sharp hooks shot from its hands. "Crush! Mush! Destroy!"

Then its pace slowed, and its arms fell to its sides. Two feet away, it ground to a halt with a last *"rrr . . ."* The robot's red eyes winked out.

"It worked!" I cried. "I'm a genius!"

"Oh, sure," said Natalie, "if most geniuses are barely passing math class."

I surveyed the roomful of battling 'bots. "Natalie, there's too many of 'em. How do we dump soup on all those droids?"

"Leave that to me."

Natalie flapped her wings and sailed over the crowd to the stage, where the Stench Bombs had finally stopped playing. In one smooth move, she swooped down and snatched the microphone off its stand.

"Robots, hear me!" she boomed in her best Oliver impression. "Everyone to the back of the room for refueling. Move it!"

At their creator's voice, the robots stopped their rampage. "*Bzzz,* yesmaster," they droned, and began rolling toward me.

The Stench Bombs started after Natalie, who jerked the mike cord from its amplifier and flew away with it.

Near the front of the room, Oliver waved his wings like a wannabe cheerleader. He was trying to catch the robots' attention, but only a few heard him over the din. The rest lined up obediently at the refreshment table.

I dipped and splattered, dipped and splattered as the line advanced—although it broke my heart to waste all that food.

Waldo the furball joined me. Brown soup splashed everywhere. By the time we'd dosed all the droids, I was painted in it from head to foot, like a gumbo gecko.

"Good job, Chet!" said Waldo.

Misty-eyed, I licked my soggy sleeve. "Good soup, Waldo."

One by one, the droids ran down. Following my

example, some teachers had taken the last of the gumbo—oh, the waste!—and cornered Oliver and the remaining robots.

The rest was just mopping up. Literally. (I licked up as much as I could.)

Before long, the teachers had hauled off Oliver's gang—which included Sarah Tonin, Trixie, and the Stench Bombs.

T-Bone, it turned out, was just a dupe. Trixie had conned him.

"See, she told T-Bone the blackmail letter was a school report for Ms. Shrewer," I said to Natalie after I got the scoop.

"So he wasn't framing me after all," she said.

"Nope. It was just your bad luck that Ms. Shrewer caught you picking up the letter."

Natalie pointed toward the door. "And it's just T-Bone's bad luck that he's hot stuff with the ladies."

I looked. Anne Gwish was leading the ringtail away. Poor sucker.

Natalie and I slumped into folding chairs, exhausted.

"I'm too pooped to pop," she said.

"I'll never feel the same way about vacuum cleaners again," I said.

As I stared at the floor, a pair of paws in brown pumps stepped into view.

"Ahem," said a battery-acid voice.

"'Ahem'?" I said, looking at my partner.

"That's what she said," said Natalie. "'Ahem.'"

We looked up. The sour vice principal, Ms. Shrewer, stood before us. She looked even more bitter than usual, like she'd just eaten a lemon-and-liverwurst sandwich.

"I, er..." She glanced at Principal Zero, who nodded. "I apologize for suspending you, Miss Attired," said the shrew in the tightest, smallest voice imaginable.

Natalie gaped.

Ms. Shrewer looked as if two particularly nasty bugs had just crawled up her nostrils. She shuddered and turned to go, but Mr. Zero shook his head.

"And as the real blackmailers have been apprehended, thanks in part to you," she said, "I'm suspending your suspension. Be back at school on Monday."

I clapped Natalie on the back. "Way to go, partner."

"Th-thank you, ma'am," she stammered to the vice principal.

"Say, Ms. Shrewer," I said, "I was wondering."

The shrew eyed me. "Yes?"

"What exactly did Oliver have on you, anyway?"

"I, er, used to be a dancer."

"A cancan dancer," said Mr. Zero, "by the name of Fifi L'Amour."

Her glare could've melted a cement vest. "Tell anyone, and you die."

"Mum's the word," I said, "Fifi."

With a mighty effort, Natalie and I smothered our smiles. We rose and shuffled out the door, leaving the scowling shrew behind.

The late-afternoon sun turned the treetops golden, and kids were piling into cars, headed home. Behind us, Maureen DeBree was removing batteries and piling robots into a recycling bin.

We moseyed across the parking lot.

"What do you think will happen to Oliver?" said Natalie.

"Ah, they'll probably send him to a school for the criminally gifted—the kind with bars on the windows and recess in a concrete courtyard."

She grinned. "I'd much rather be at Emerson Hicky. Thanks, Chet."

"Aw, forget it," I said. "After all, what are friends for?"

"To eat the last of your Katydid Chunk bars?"

I smiled. "Now that you mention it, birdie, snacks at your house?"

As we headed down the street, Natalie cocked her head. "Say, Chet, have you heard the one about the two friends and the missing nostril tweezers?"

"As a matter of fact, birdie," I said, "I have. But tell it again anyway."

Look for more mysteries from
the Tattered Casebook of Chet Gecko
in hardcover and paperback

Case #1 *The Chameleon Wore Chartreuse*

Some cases start rough, some cases start easy. This one started with a dame. (That's what we private eyes call a girl.) She was cute and green and scaly. She looked like trouble and smelled like . . . grasshoppers.

Shirley Chameleon came to me when her little brother, Billy, turned up missing. (I suspect she also came to spread cooties, but that's another story.) She turned on the tears. She promised me some stinkbug pie. I said I'd find the brat.

But when his trail led to a certain stinky-breathed, bad-tempered, jumbo-sized Gila monster, I thought I'd bitten off more than I could chew. Worse, I had to chew fast: If I didn't find Billy in time, it would be bye-bye, stinkbug pie.

Case #2 *The Mystery of Mr. Nice*

How would you know if some criminal mastermind tried to impersonate your principal? My first clue: He was nice to me.

This fiend tried everything—flattery, friendship, food—but he still couldn't keep me off the case. Natalie and I followed a trail of clues as thin as the cheese on a cafeteria hamburger. And we found a ring of corruption that went from the janitor right up to Mr. Big.

In the nick of time, we rescued Principal Zero and busted up the PTA meeting, putting a stop to the evil genius. And what thanks did we get? Just the usual. A cold handshake and a warm soda.

But that's all in a day's work for a private eye.

Case #3   *Farewell, My Lunchbag*

If danger is my business, then dinner is my passion. I'll take any case if the pay is right. And what pay could be better than Mothloaf Surprise?

At least that's what I thought. But in this particular case, I bit off more than I could chew.

Cafeteria lady Mrs. Bagoong hired me to track down whoever was stealing her food supplies. The long, slimy trail led too close to my own backyard for comfort.

And much, much too close to my old archenemy, Jimmy "King" Cobra. Without the help of Natalie Attired and our school janitor, Maureen DeBree, I would've been gecko sushi.

Case #4   *The Big Nap*

My grades were lower than a salamander's slippers, and my bank account was trying to crawl under a duck's belly. So why did I take a case that didn't pay anything?

Put it this way: Would *you* stand by and watch some

evil power turn *your* classmates into hypnotized zombies? (If that wasn't just what normally happened to them in math class, I mean.)

My investigations revealed a plot meaner than a roomful of rhinos with diaper rash.

Someone at Emerson Hicky was using a sinister video game to put more and more students into la-la-land. And it was up to me to stop it, pronto—before that someone caught up with me, and I found myself taking the Big Nap.

Case #5 *The Hamster of the Baskervilles*

Elementary school is a wild place. But this was ridiculous.

Someone—or some*thing*—was tearing up Emerson Hicky. Classrooms were trashed. Walls were gnawed. Mysterious tunnels riddled the playground like worm chunks in a pan of earthworm lasagna.

But nobody could spot the culprit, let alone catch him.

I don't believe in the supernatural. My idea of voodoo is my mom's cockroach-ripple ice cream.

Then, a teacher reported seeing a monster on full-moon night, and I got the call.

At the end of a twisted trail of clues, I had to answer the burning question: Was it a vicious, supernatural were-hamster on the loose, or just another Science Fair project gone wrong?

Case #6 *This Gum for Hire*

Never thought I'd see the day when one of my worst enemies would hire me for a case. Herman the Gila Monster was a sixth-grade hoodlum with a first-rate left hook. He told me someone was disappearing the football team, and he had to put a stop to it. *Big whoop.*

He told me he was being blamed for the kidnappings, and he had to clear his name. *Boo hoo.*

Then he said that I could either take the case and earn a nice reward, or have my face rearranged like a bargain-basement Picasso painted by a spastic chimp.

I took the case.

But before I could find the kidnapper, I had to go undercover. And that meant facing something that scared me worse than a chorus line of criminals in steel-toed boots: P.E. class.

Case #7 *The Malted Falcon*

It was tall, dark, and chocolatey—the stuff dreams are made of. It was a treat so titanic that nobody had been able to finish one single-handedly (or even single-mouthedly). It was the Malted Falcon.

How far would you go for the ultimate dessert? Somebody went too far, and that's where I came in.

The local sweets shop held a contest. The prize: a year's supply of free Malted Falcons. Some lucky kid scored the winning ticket. She brought it to school for show-and-tell.

But after she showed it, somebody swiped it. And no one would tell where it went.

Following a strong hunch and an even stronger sweet tooth, I tracked the ticket through a web of lies more tangled than a rattlesnake doing the rumba. But the time to claim the prize was fast approaching. Would the villain get the sweet treat—or his just desserts?

Case #8   *Trouble Is My Beeswax*

Okay, I confess. When test time rolls around, I'm as tempted as the next lizard to let my eyeballs do the walking . . . to my neighbor's paper.

But Mrs. Gecko didn't raise no cheaters. (Some language manglers, perhaps.) So when a routine investigation uncovered a test-cheating ring at Emerson Hicky, I gave myself a new case: Put the cheaters out of business.

Easier said than done. Those double-dealers were slicker than a frog's fanny and twice as slimy.

Oh, and there was one other small problem: The finger of suspicion pointed to two dames. The ringleader was either the glamorous Lacey Vail, or my own classmate Shirley Chameleon.

Sheesh. The only thing I hate worse than an empty Pillbug Crunch wrapper is a case full of dizzy dames.

Case #9   *Give My Regrets to Broadway*

Some things you can't escape, however hard you try—like dentist appointments, visits with strange-smelling relatives, and being in the fourth-grade play. I had always left the acting to my smart-aleck pal, Natalie, but then one day it was my turn in the spotlight.

Stage fright? Me? You're talking about a gecko who has laughed at danger, chuckled at catastrophe, and sneezed at sinister plots.

I was terrified.

Not because of the acting, mind you. The script called for me to share a major lip-lock with Shirley Chameleon—Cootie Queen of the Universe!

And while I was trying to avoid that trap, a simple missing-persons case took a turn for the worse—right into the middle of my play. Would opening night spell curtains for my client? And, more important, would someone invent a cure for cooties? But no matter—whatever happens, the sleuth must go on.